Legal

I0618272

ISBN: 978-1-7321877-4-0

This publication is designed to provide accurate and authoritative information in regard to the subject matter covered. It is sold with the understanding that neither the author nor the publisher is engaged in rendering legal, accounting, or other professional service. If legal advice or other expert assistance is required, the services of a competent professional person should be sought.

--From a Declaration of Principles Jointly Adopted by a Committee of the American Bar Association and a Committee of Publishers and Associations.

The views and opinions expressed herein are those of the author alone and do not reflect the views of any university, employers, former employers and/or their affiliates.

Table of Contents

Introduction

I recently discovered the prototype for *The Book About the Crystal World* sifting through the archives. This text was written when I was in secondary school and the year was 1986 and I was in the 6th or 7th grade. This notebook was one of my early forays into science fiction, space flight, ninjas and character development. Designing my own symbol-language (included below), time travel and other dimensions fascinated me.

I was always trying entrepreneurial things, selling my mom's homemade pizza in the 3rd grade by diving up the slices and re-selling them to my classmates. I also sold lemonade to the university students in front of my house.

I am bringing back the characters in *The Book About the Crystal World* in a comic book series. This will be complimented by a second concurrent comic book series of early action figures that I also developed.

Finally I will be releasing my first fiction novel, based on covert operations and the underworld.

Without further adieu, here is the first time-capsule release, complete with a long complicated title.

CYRSTAL WORLD

The Book About the Cyrstal World

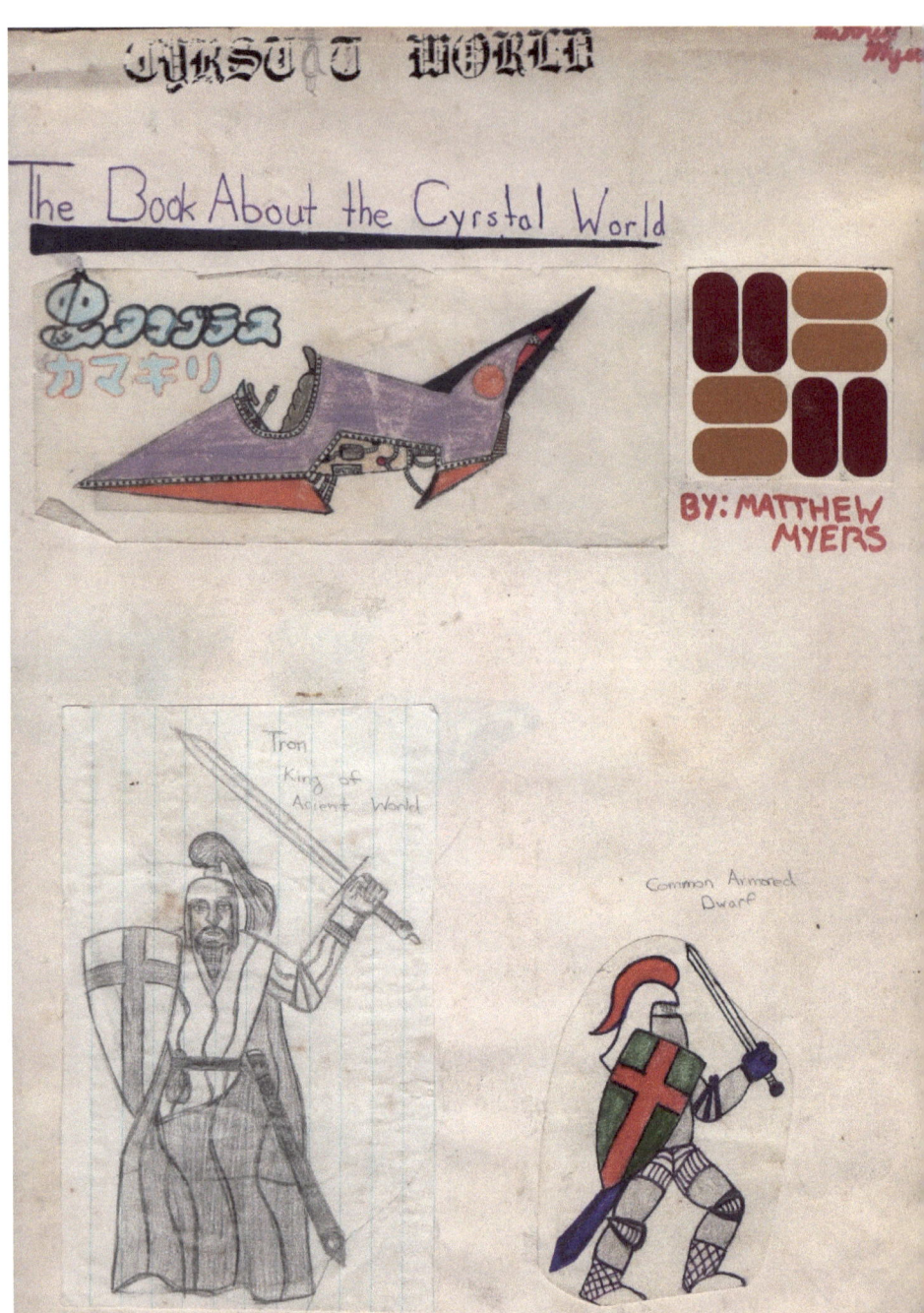

カマキリ

BY: MATTHEW MYERS

Tron
King of
Ancient World

Common Armored
Dwarf

タマゴマンデス M-4カマキリ星

タマゴを始めさせてください。

Warriors

M-3

Man: Zonk 1.2
Weapons: Lazer Eyes
Rank: 8

Man: Sunman 2.5005
Weapons: Two-Handed Swords
Rank: 10

カミキリムシ ♯
YOZK 1.2

カミキリムシ 軽量カミキリム神
SUNMAN 2.5005

Driver: VEGA YULA ●
Ship: Moonstruck 0.2
Speed: 1500 miles per hour
Size: 72 feet
Length: 12 feet ▲
Wingspan: 6 feet
Hieght: 3 feet

Ships + Space Ships

TYPE OF SHIP: MOON 0.2

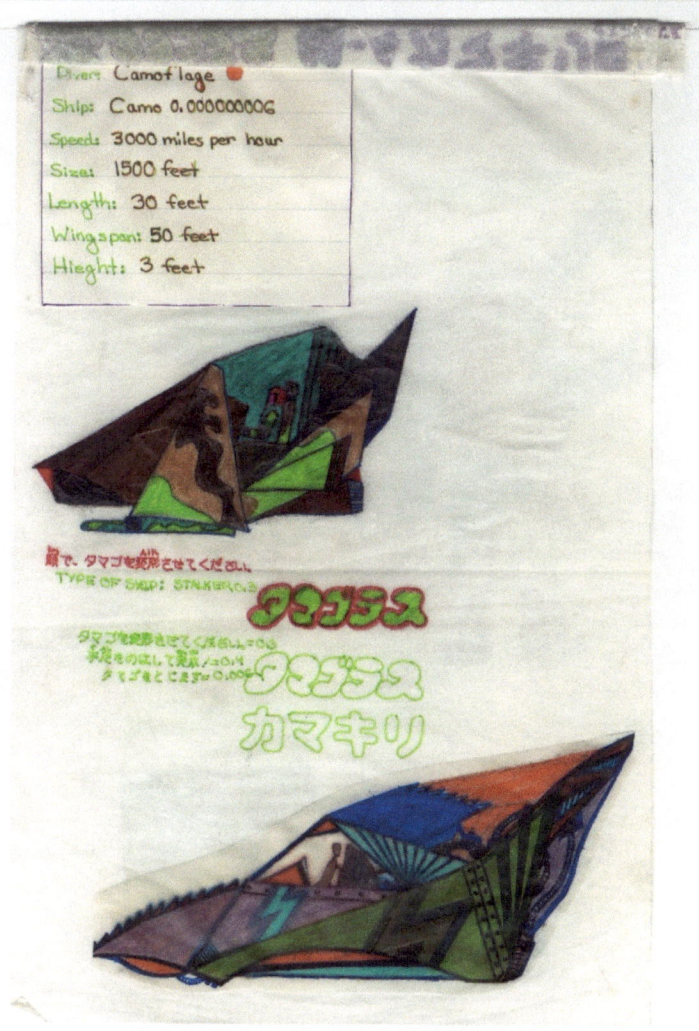

River: Camoflage
Ship: Camo 0.00000000G
Speed: 3000 miles per hour
Size: 1500 feet
Length: 30 feet
Wingspan: 50 feet
Hieght: 3 feet

翼で、タマゴを変形させてください。
TYPE OF SHIP: STALKER(?)

タゴラス

タマゴを変形させてくださいての
糸庭をのばして変示ノコ0.4
タミゴきとにきます0.00

タゴラス

カマキリ

Maps

Modern World

Water Gate

Un-Inhibited Land

ZORK

Pit of Zork

City of Zork

Grassland

BLACK SEAS

Pit of Fire

The

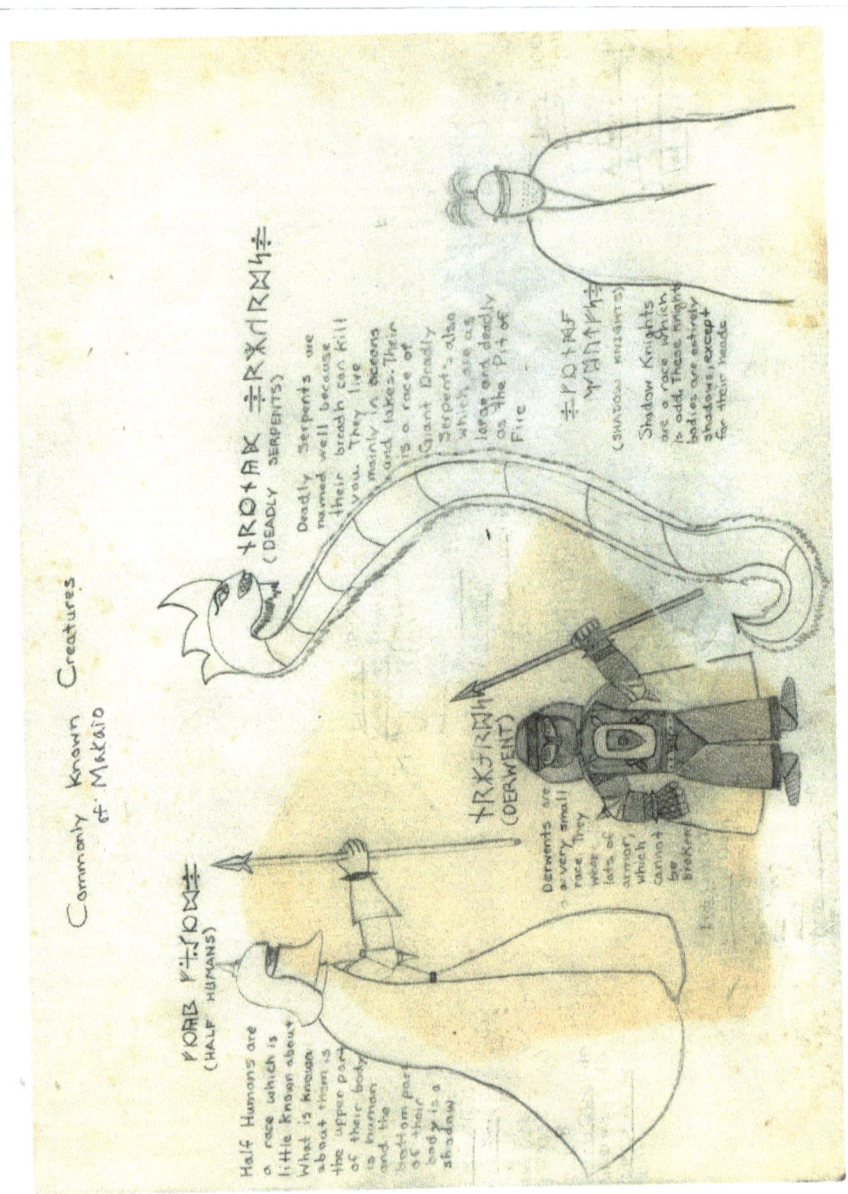

Commonly Known Creatures of Makaio

ᚦOᛗB ᚠᛁᛊOᚾᚦ
(HALF HUMANS)

Half Humans are a race which is little known about. What is known about them is the upper part of their body is human and the bottom part of their body is a shadow

ᛏᚱOᛏᚪK ᚦᚱᚾᚪᚱᛗᚾᚦ
(DEADLY SERPENTS)

Deadly Serpents are named well because their breath can kill you. They live mainly in oceans and lakes. Their is a race of Giant Deadly Serpents, also which are as large and deadly as the Pit of Fire

ᛏᚱᚾᛊᚱᛗᚾᛁᚪ
(DERWENT)

Derwents are a very small race. They wield lots of armor, which cannot be broken

ᚦᚱOᛏᚾᚠ ᚤᚪᚾᚦᚪᚠᛁᚷ
(SHADOW KNIGHTS)

Shadow Knights are a race which it said. These toungish bodies are entirely shadows, except for their heads

Rare Creatures of Makaio

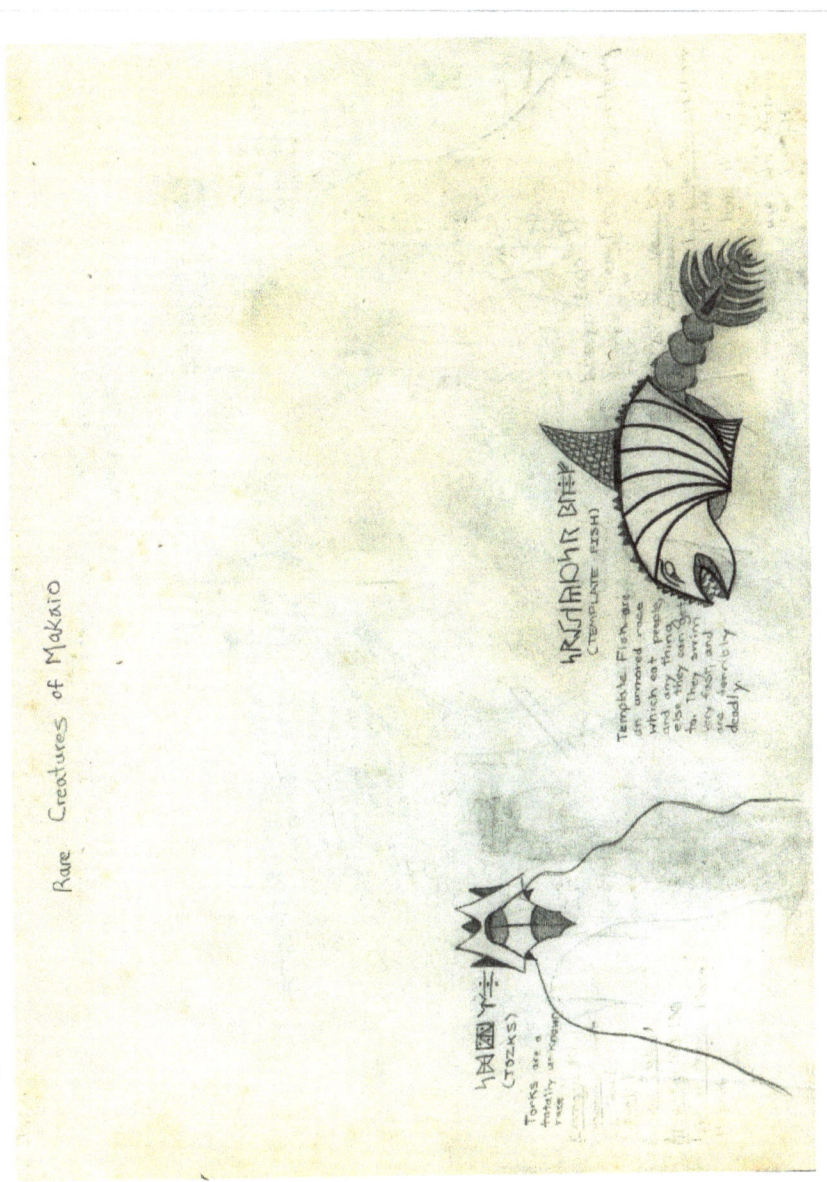

ᚻᚱᚲᛗᛁᚑᚻᚱ ᛒᚻᛃᚤ
(TEMPLATE FISH)

Temple Fish are
an armored race
which eat people
and anything
else they can get
to. They swim
very fast and
are terribly
deadly.

ᚻᛈᛚ ᚷᚤᛉ
(TORKS)

Torks are a
totally unknown
race.

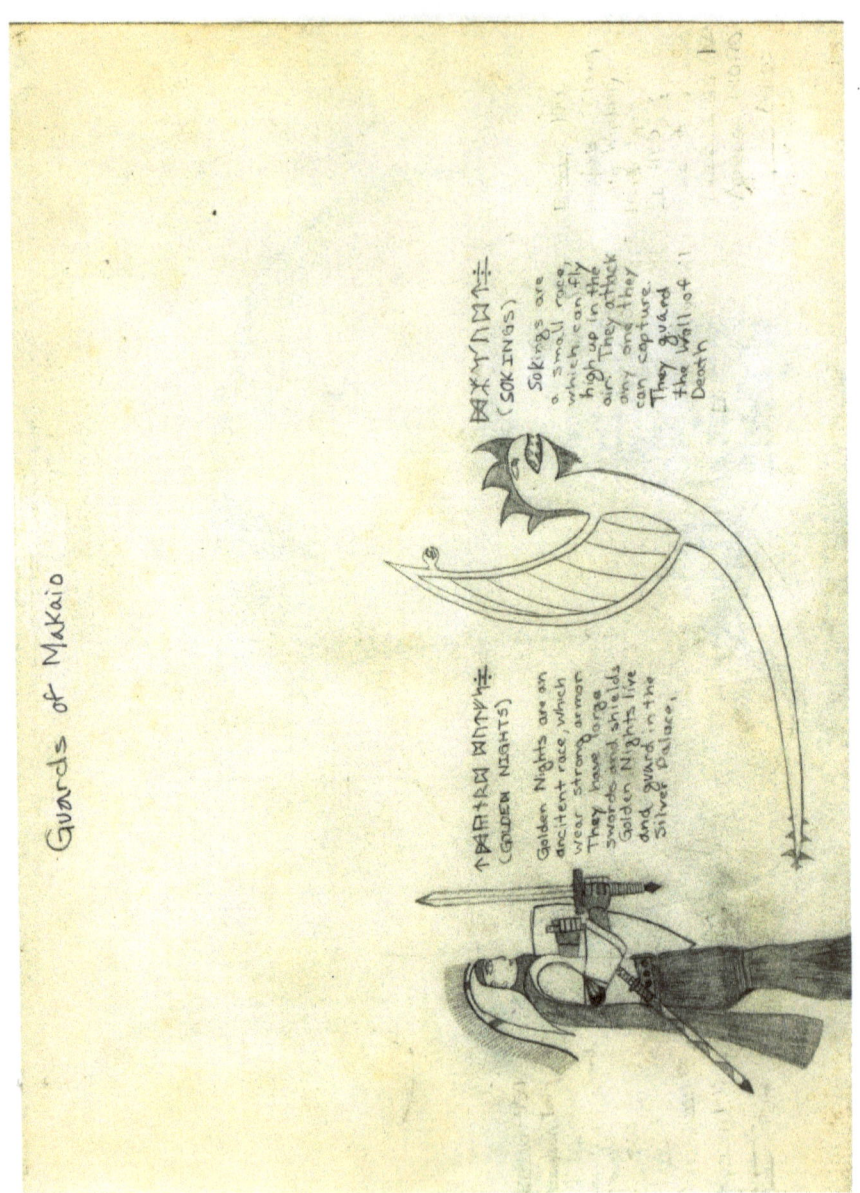

Guards of Makaio

(GOLDEN NIGHTS)

Golden Nights are an ancient race, which wear strong armor. They have large swords and shields. Golden Nights live and guard in the Silver Palace.

(SOKINGS)

Sokings are a small race which can fly high up in the air. They attack any one they can capture. They guard the Wall of Death.

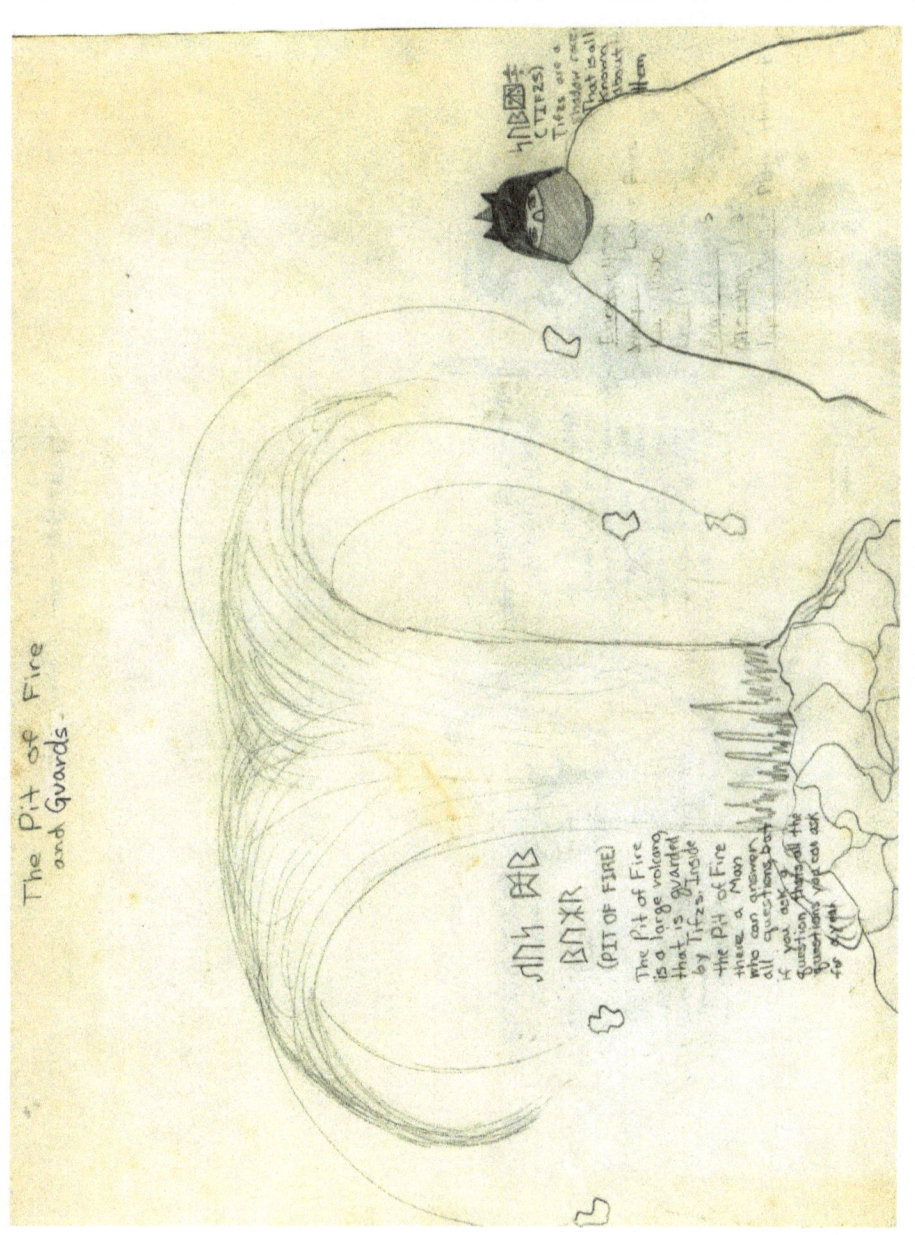

The Pit of Fire and Guards.

Unknown Forest Creatures

Maps & Language

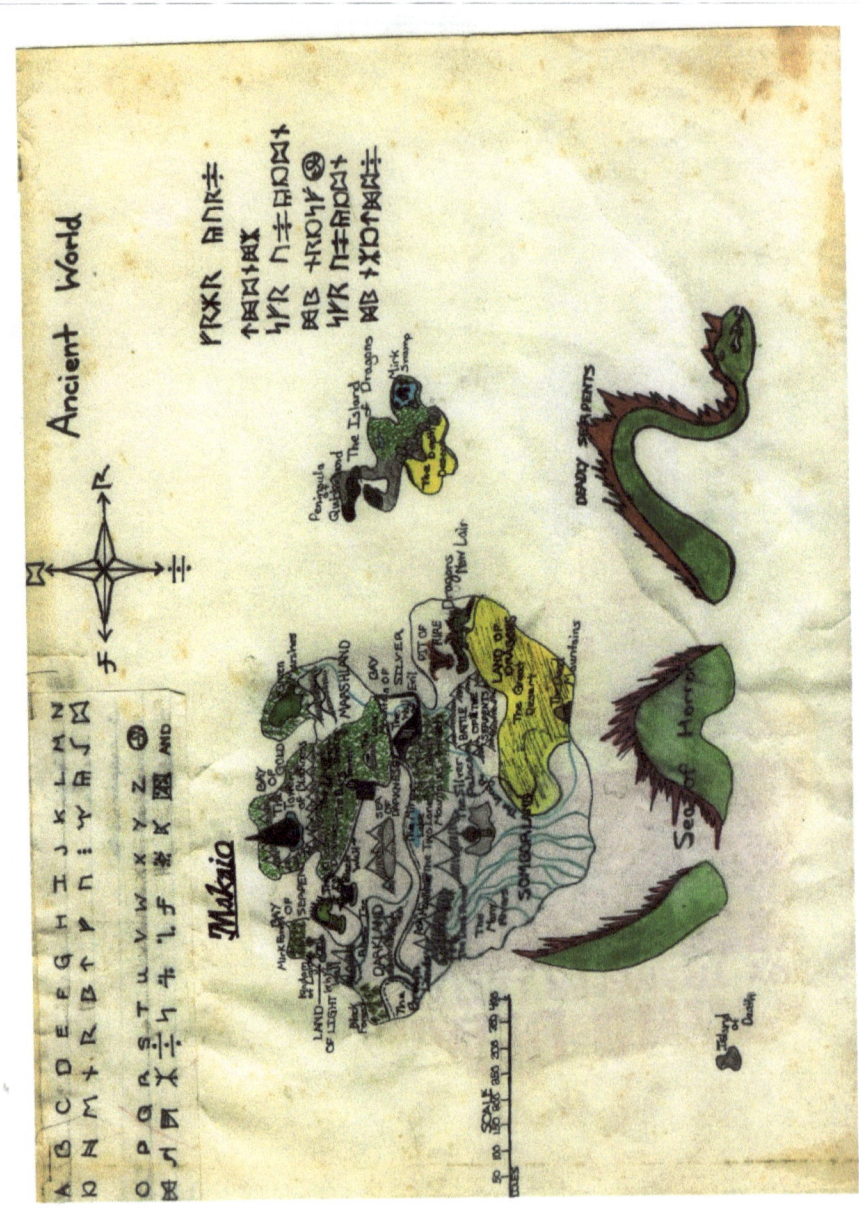

Ancient World

Mukaia

Time Travel

5 Dimensions of Makaio

1. line

2. flat square

3. Box

4. time

5. vessel/trac — First

   Second

2nd Language

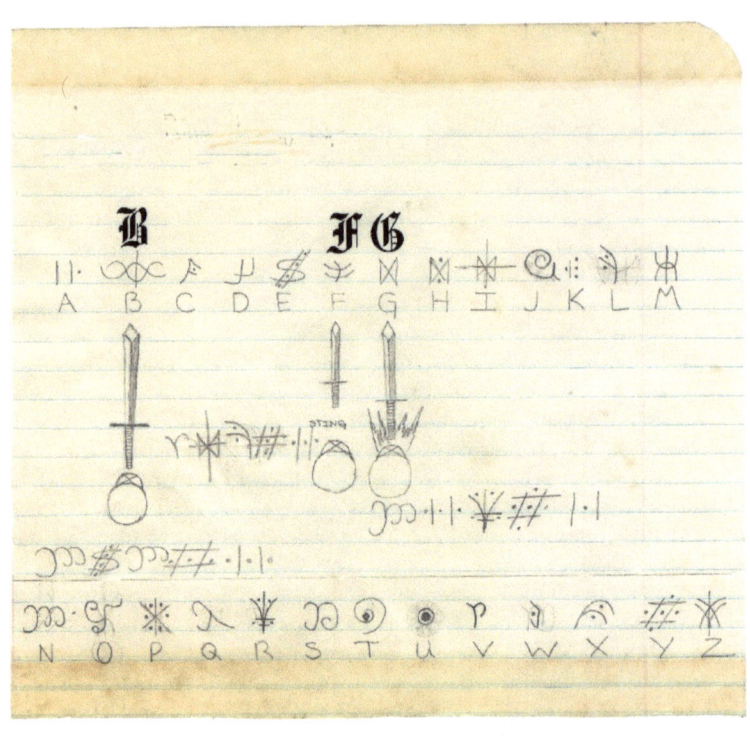

24

Game

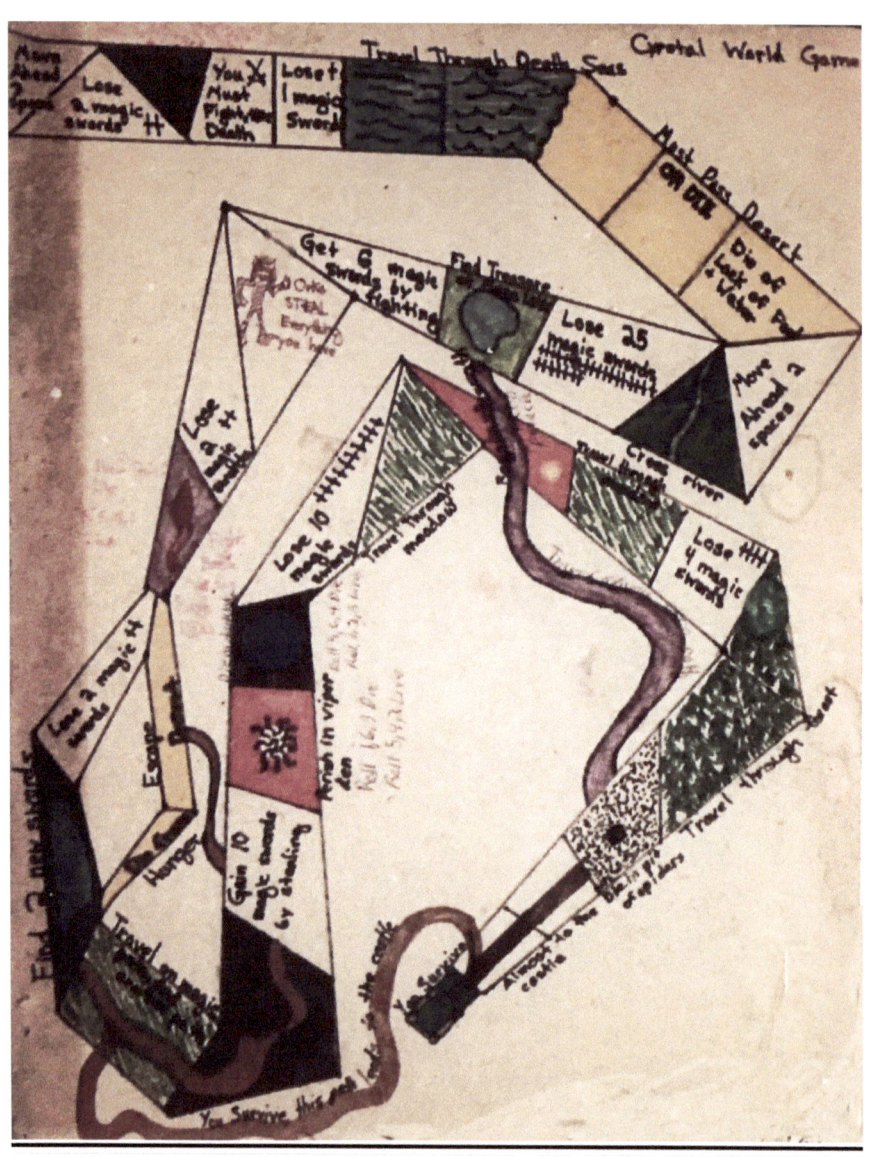

www.ingramcontent.com/pod-product-compliance
Lightning Source LLC
Chambersburg PA
CBHW040312180626
46815CB00016B/299

9 781732 187740